It's Okay to Ask

My name is Temi,
short for Temistocles.

I know it's an unusual name,
perhaps one you've never heard
before.
That's why I like it; it makes me
feel special and unique.

For as long as I can remember, I have had the desire to get
to know the world around me.
I wanted to know all the answers to the questions that
popped into my head.

Some of these questions, I answered myself.
By sitting down, observing the world, and listening,
I got to understand what was going on around me.

Still, there were some questions too deep for me to understand, all by myself.

So, I started looking for those answers by asking the grownups I knew.

"Mom, why do we have to go to school?"

"Because I said so," Mom replied.

"But why?" I genuinely wanted to know.

"That's just the way it is," she said, "that's why."

Hmm, I guess sometimes I won't get answers to the questions I have.

But if going to school is important to grownups, then school must be important.

And just like that, I started creating my conclusions
about the way that the world worked.

Like when I asked my mom,

"Why did the world begin?"

She gave me a simple answer: "It just did. Sometimes, you don't have to think of the why's of the world, just accept things as they are."

I accepted this answer, even though it didn't feel quite right. Mom was a grownup; she must know everything.

One day at school, we learned about dinosaurs, monkeys, cavemen, and the evolution of human beings.

I got curious and confused!

I wanted to know the why's.

So, I asked my teacher if she knew why human beings were created.

She said there was no need for the class to know the answer to that question.

Now, I was even more confused!

When I got home, I decided to ask my dad. He said he was too tired and had no time for silly questions.

What was silly about this question?

And why were grownups always tired?

Being a grownup didn't seem fun at all!

I realized...

Grownups didn't know everything.

Grownups said stuff without knowing why they said it.

Grownups had less energy than children.

I knew why I asked those questions — I was curious and eager.

Why didn't grownups want to know the truths about the world they were living in?

Perhaps my parents and my teacher were not old enough to know all the answers to my questions.

I'd have to ask my great-grandfather.
He must know everything by now.

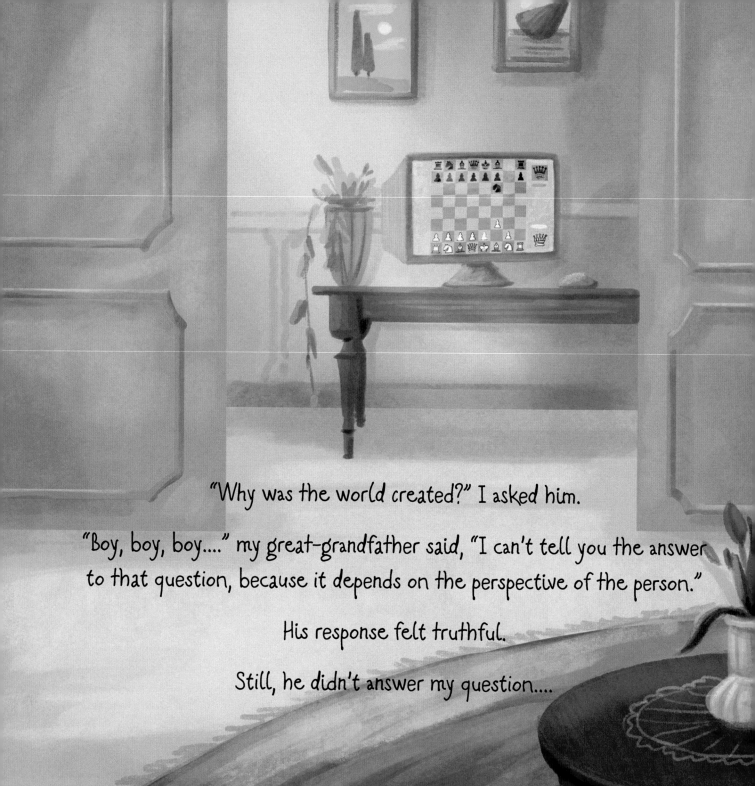

"Why was the world created?" I asked him.

"Boy, boy, boy...." my great-grandfather said, "I can't tell you the answer to that question, because it depends on the perspective of the person."

His response felt truthful.

Still, he didn't answer my question....

I decided to ask one more grownup...
But I'd have to pick the right one.

Gustavo, my great-grandfather's driver! He always had a smile on his face, perhaps because he knew some of the answers to my questions about the world.

"What is 'perspective'?" I asked.

"Perspective is the unique view every person has," he told me with a gleam in his eye. "Every single human being sees, feels, and thinks differently. For example, the word **dream** in Spanish is written **sueño**. It has different letters, but the same meaning. So, too, can be the views we have of the world. A different perspective to the same story."

I surely picked the right person!

"Why was the world created?" I continued.

"Nobody knows," Gustavo explained. "What we do know is that we are here, and certainly there is a purpose for that."

"How come nobody knows?" I asked.

"People have many theories," he said, "but the truth is, there are still a lot of answers yet to be found. It takes curious people like you, to question the why's and find the answers for the world."

"How can I know the truth if we all have different views?" I asked.

"By being *you*: curious, open, smart, enthusiastic, authentic, brave, playful, honest, and connected to your feelings. You see, the truth is you. It's what feels right inside. We all are a unique piece in this big puzzle we call the world. You are giving your truth to the world, by being you."

"Why do grownups stop questioning the why's of the world?"
I wanted to know.

"Grown-ups may be afraid of the unknown, afraid of making mistakes, or of showing their unique perspectives to the world, even though our different answers are the ones that when pieced together create the truths of the world."

Gustavo continued, "The people who do wonder about the why's, are the ones that make the world a better place.

When grownups tell you their answers, check inside, and if it feels right, then it is your truth now."

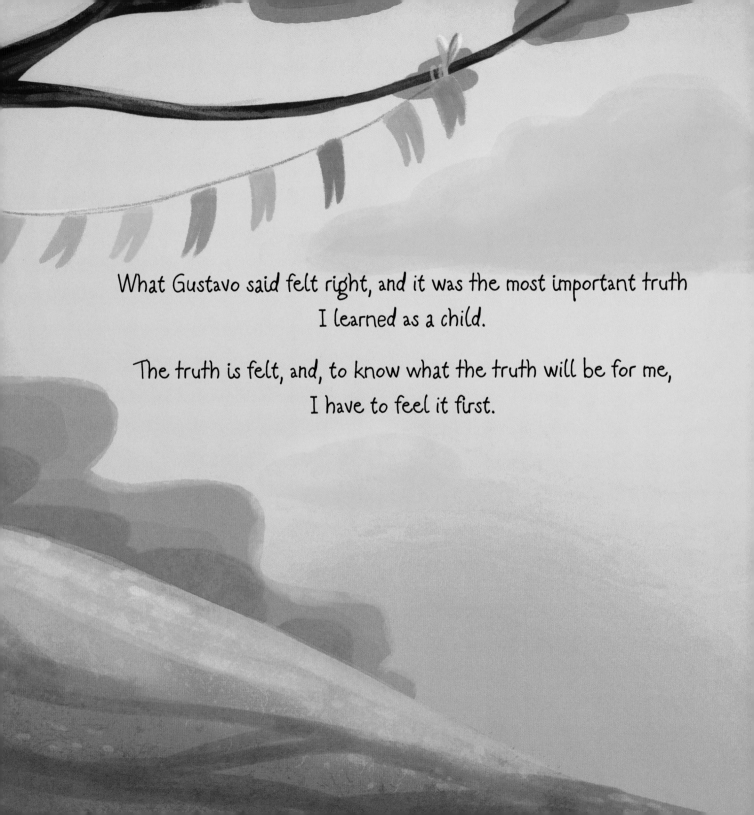

What Gustavo said felt right, and it was the most important truth
I learned as a child.

The truth is felt, and, to know what the truth will be for me,
I have to feel it first.

It's okay to ask the why's....
Not all grownups are tired....
Everyone is unique....
There is a purpose for that uniqueness....

Why are we here in the world?

TO BE OURSELVES!

ABOUT THE AUTHOR

Temi Díaz is a writer, film producer, and entrepreneur from Panama City, Panama. He recently created Inner Truth Books to strengthen children and adults' emotional intelligence through stories that teach self-empowerment, values, authenticity, empathy, and more. The author truly believes everyone is unique in this world, so it is essential for kids to conserve their authenticity and for adults to get back to it to achieve their fullest potential.

Made in the USA
Monee, IL
30 August 2021